BUSY BEA

For Jane Feder

Margaret K. McElderry Books
Macmillan Publishing Company
866 Third Avenue
New York, NY 10022

Maxwell Macmillan Canada, Inc.
1200 Eglinton Avenue East
Suite 200
Don Mills, Ontario M3C 3N1

Macmillan Publishing Company is part of the Maxwell Communication Group of Companies.
First edition
Printed in Hong Kong by South China Printing Company (1988) Ltd.
10 9 8 7 6 5 4 3 2 1
The text of this book is set in Revival 565 BT.
The illustrations are rendered in watercolor.
Library of Congress Cataloging-in-Publication Data
Poydar, Nancy.
Busy Bea / Nancy Poydar. — 1st ed.
p.   cm.
Summary: Bea is too busy to keep track of her own belongings but she
always knows just where things are for her grandmother.
ISBN 0-689-50592-2
[1. Lost and found possessions—Fiction. 2. Grandmothers—Fiction.]
I. Title.
PZ7.P8846Bu 1994
[E]—dc20
93-37266

Busy Bea

Nancy Poydar

MARGARET K. McELDERRY BOOKS
New York
Maxwell Macmillan Canada
Toronto
Maxwell Macmillan International
New York Oxford Singapore Sydney

Bea was always losing her belongings. It wasn't because she was careless. It was because she was such a busy person.

On the first day of school she almost forgot to take her lunch box.

Later in the day she lost it.

On a warm afternoon Bea left her jacket somewhere.

Another day her raincoat was missing.

Bea's mama frowned. "Your lunch box, your jacket, and now your raincoat! If your nose wasn't stuck to the middle of your face, you'd forget that too."

But Grandma promised that their busy Bea would outgrow this forgetting business. "Bea always helps me find things," she said. And she was right. Bea could find Grandma's glasses in no time at all.

On the next rainy day, Bea had to carry her papa's umbrella to school, because she had lost her raincoat, but when it was time to go home—

Bea forgot it.

Bea felt bad. Mama was frustrated. "Your lunch box, your jacket, your raincoat, and now your papa's umbrella!"

But soon Bea was too busy finding Grandma's missing knitting needle to worry about the forgetting business.

Grandma smiled. "What would I do without our busy Bea to find things for me? Bea, look hard at school and I'm sure you'll find your lost things."

Meanwhile, Mama wrote a note for Bea to take to her teacher.

But the next morning Bea lost the note.

After school Mama declared, "Bea, you amaze me. Your lunch box, your jacket, your raincoat, your papa's umbrella, and now the note!

"If your ears weren't stuck to the sides of your head, you'd forget them too."

Soon Bea was too busy finding Grandma's knitting basket to think about the forgetting business.

"I have something in the basket for you, Bea," Grandma said, "for helping me find things all the time."

But the very next morning Bea was so busy getting an empty bird's nest to bring into school that she left her new sweater . . . somewhere.

After school Bea was too busy

looking for her new sweater

to go home.

When Bea told her teacher about the missing sweater, the teacher
asked, "Have you been too busy to notice our lost-and-found?"

When Bea got home at last, Mama smiled. "Bea, you do amaze me!"

Right away Bea was busy finding Grandma, so Grandma could enjoy
the surprise.

But Grandma wasn't surprised at all.